# SAM

---

## EYE CANDY INK #3

### SHAW HART

## BLURB

Sam Kavan has grown up learning to be tough, at least on the outside. Raised by her dad and two brothers, she's always seemed to fit in more as one of the guys. Maybe that's why she's seen as either one of the boys or as a little sister. When she moves to Pittsburgh and starts at Eye Candy Ink, she fits in perfectly and soon she's found another family in the men who work at the shop with her.

Like everyone else at the shop, she's not interested in falling in love. In fact, after a string of failed dates, she's sick of dating. She doesn't want to go out with boys who send her dick pics or who text at midnight looking to hook up. She wants someone that she can rely on — Someone who loves and wants her for her.

She wants a real man.

Then she meets Maxwell Schulz, and she wonders if she can survive a real man.

# 1

## S am

WHY ARE GUYS SUCH IDIOTS?

No, seriously, it's a legitimate question. I've been trying to get Nico's last client to leave for about ten minutes now but he's still leaning on the front counter, blabbering on about lord only knows what. I tuned him out as soon as he said I was pretty. He's already paid so there's no reason for him to still be here and if he bothered to pay attention to anyone but himself, then he would have noticed that I am clearly not interested.

"So, then I was like, 'Liam, bro, you can't have a green rover because I already called it.'

He rolls his eyes at me like I should find his buddy Liam just as ridiculous as he does and I just stare blankly back at him. *Get the hell out,* I mentally scream at him. He ignores my obviously disinterested face and goes on.

I've seen this type of guy before and I can already see what would happen if I went home with him. His place would be small, his bedroom littered with dirty socks and underwear and smelling like stale beer. There are probably at least two posters of half-naked women draped over cars tacked up in his room and his bed is unmade with sheets that have probably never been washed. He'll get off in under twenty minutes, leaving me dissatisfied and then I'll pretend like I had a great time and get the hell out of there. In a day or two, I'll get a text at midnight with a picture of his dick and an invite to come over and sit on it. I'll ignore him and pray that we never run into each other again.

My last few dates might have left me a little disillusioned and bitter.

I'm just so sick of men- no, not men. Boys. I'm so sick of going out with boys pretending to be men. Boys who have no idea what they want or who they are, let alone how to treat a woman. This guy yammering on about who the hell cares? He is most definitely a boy.

I sigh, loudly, and the guy waiting in the chair by the door laughs. He came in a couple of minutes ago but I haven't been able to find out who he's here to see because I can't get rid of Chad here.

That guy? Oh, he's all man. He's hot and I'd guess he's in his mid-thirties with pitch black hair and bright green eyes. He's fit and I glance quickly at where he's sprawled out in the chair. He's got one big booted foot resting on his knee and a white button-down shirt tucked into dark blue jeans. The sleeves of his shirt are rolled up and I think I see a tattoo on his forearm but I force my eyes away before I stare too long.

Don't want him to get the wrong idea. My brothers taught me the best way to get rid of boys when I was younger. Just ignore them and if that doesn't work, then tell them to get lost. Most guys think you're a bitch if you tell them point blank that you're not interested but those are also the guys who can't take cues from body language so they obviously need it spelled out for them.

I grew up in Buffalo, New York with my dad and two older brothers. My mom passed away when I was five. Cancer. It sucked but at least I got to spend some time with her. My dad and brothers did their best to fill the hole she left in our family and I'll always love them for that. My dad was a boxer before he had kids. Once we came along, he stopped and started training other guys instead. He has a gym in downtown Buffalo and I remember spending most of my time helping out there.

I thought one of my brothers would grow up and become a boxer or fighter too but they chose different paths. Miles, the oldest of us, became a police officer, and Abe became a firefighter.

Being raised by three guys was interesting and I know that they were definitely overprotective. They were supportive when I told them that I wanted to become a body piercer, probably because I would have a lot of needles to use as weapons if I needed to. I had originally wanted to be a tattoo artist but I'm not the best drawer. When I went to the local tattoo parlor and saw the piercing charts, I fell in love.

They were decidedly less happy when I told them that I was moving to Pittsburgh. You would have thought it was the end of the world. I had to promise that I would call every week and come visit at least once a month. They've gotten more relaxed on that after they met the guys at Eye Candy Ink and saw that I had found a group of guys who were going to love and protect me like family.

Atlas and I met when we were interviewed by Zeke and we grew closer as friends as we explored the city together. He's such a sweetheart that it was hard not to love him. Mischa would join us half of the time and it's impossible not to like that guy. He might drive you crazy sometimes with his antics but inside, he's a puppy dog. Nico and Zeke are both older and have been tattooing for over a decade. They're both masters at it and I love watching them work, although Zeke rarely does it these days. Nico lets me sit in on some of his sessions though and he never minds if I flip through some of his drawing pads. The guy is such a talented dude. He could have been a painter or something and made it big but he loves tattoos.

I look back to the guy in the chair and see he's still watching me, a slight smile on his lips. I wonder if Nico has one last client tonight. *I wouldn't mind sitting in on his session*, I think as my eyes run over the guy once again. I catch myself when my eyes start to linger and jerk my gaze away and back to Chad. It's time to get this loser the hell out of here.

I sigh again and straighten my shoulders, pushing some of my freshly dyed hair away from my face. I dye it a different color every few weeks. This time it's a bright fire engine red that you can see from a mile away. I found this pair of Converse that were the same color and fell in love. I wiggle my toes in my shoes as my eyes meet Chad's.

"Well, thanks for coming in," I say, cutting him off.

I'm at work after all so I can't be too rude.

Chad breaks off mid-sentence and seems genuinely surprised that someone would dare to interrupt him. I want to roll my eyes at that but instead I just paste my most professional, bland smile on my face.

"Yeah, so anyways," Chad starts, his eyes trailing down to

my tight black Eye Candy Ink shirt. I roll my eyes at that but he's not looking at my face so he misses it.

"Hey, asshole, my eyes are up here."

I hear a laugh behind me and turn to see Zeke standing there watching me. He should be pissed that I just talked to a customer like that but instead he just seems amused and I know that he has my back. Best boss ever.

"I was thinking that we should grab some drinks sometime," Chad says, not deterred by me calling him an asshole or calling him out for staring at my tits.

I stare at him like he's an idiot but he just looks at me expectantly. I'm pretty sure he expected me to fall all over myself to take him up on his offer and I bite back another eye roll. This is why I've sworn off dating. Who wants to spend time with a dumb little boy who is only interested in one thing? I promised myself no more dating boys after my last date ended in disaster. I left early but that didn't stop the guy from sending me a dick pic the next night and then texting me at midnight to see if I wanted to hook up.

My lip curls in disgust and I force myself to smile back politely at Chad.

"No thanks."

"Aw, come on, baby."

"I'm not your baby and I'm never going to date you. Get lost."

Chad's eyes narrow at me and he sneers "Stuck up bitch. I was going to do you a favor and let you ride this dick," he says, his hand grabbing his dick through his jeans.

"Hard. Pass." I enunciate and he glares back at me.

I can hear Zeke take a step closer and I notice that the guy sitting by the door stands to his feet as well.

"Fuck you, bitch," Chad spits as he turns on his heel and heads for the door.

"Not in this lifetime," I call after him as he storms out of the shop.

My eyes find their way back to the other customer and I see he's smiling at me again.

"Heartbreaker," he murmurs, that same small smile on his lips.

"Trust me, his heart wasn't involved. Just his dick."

He takes a step toward the front counter and my heart rate picks up. He's taller than I first thought and my mouth waters as I take him in from this new angle.

"You know..." he starts to say and my eyes narrow at him.

"I swear to god, if you say I would be a lot prettier if I just smiled every once in a while, that I'm going to hit you so hard that your kids will be born bruised."

He throws his head back and laughs and I hear Zeke join in as he heads to open the metal gate for the guy. The guy meets my gaze once again, his sea green eyes meeting my sky-blue ones. Confidence and power roll off of him and I can feel goosebumps start on my arms.

"Sam, this is my friend Max. Max, this is Sam."

"Nice to meet you," he says, holding his hand out to me.

"Yeah, you too."

His palm is warm and strong against mine and he squeezes mine gently before he slowly pulls back.

"Ready?" Zeke asks and Max nods at him.

"See you later," Max says to me.

"Don't count on it."

He smirks at me one last time before he follows Zeke back to his office and a shiver runs down my spine at the promise that I see in his eyes.

# 2

# M<sup>ax</sup>

I TAKE one last look back at the fiery, gorgeous, redheaded woman behind the front counter but as I suspected, she's not watching me. She's busy typing away on the computer and I smile as I turn back around. I like her already. Something about her no-nonsense attitude clicks with me. Watching her and interacting with her for that brief moment has already told me a lot about Sam. I can tell that she is a woman who knows what she wants out of life, who knows her own mind, and who doesn't take any shit from anyone. I'm the same way. I see something that I want or I have a goal and I don't rest until I've gotten it.

Usually my goal is a new restaurant or club. I opened my first restaurant with a friend right out of college. He was the backer but I ran it and did all of the work to open it. When that one was a success, my friend bought me out and I opened my second restaurant and then my third. I've opened four restaurants so far, all over Pittsburgh and just recently branched out to nightclubs. My passion will always be restaurants though.

My mom says that I love it so much because it's all a gamble. Growing up in Las Vegas, I'm well aware of gambling and betting it all. My mom says that it's in my blood. My dad was a famous poker player before he passed away but I never got a taste for the game. I prefer to make my own luck. Which is probably why I've always been so comfortable betting all of my money on one of my restaurants and its success.

My mom would say that I'm not making my own luck; I'm just trying to control everything. Growing up in Vegas with a professional poker player for a father didn't really lead to the most stable of childhoods. I can remember us living in a new house in a nice neighborhood but we moved when I was five to this shack on the outskirts of the old strip. It was run down and I had wanted to go back home but we never did. It wasn't until I was older that I learned what had happened. My father had gambled everything and lost. We were broke for a long time after that and then my dad got sick and passed away. He left us buried in even more debt. I kind of hated him for a while. He had just left, gotten off easy, while my mom and I had to work hard and bust our asses to make ends meet. All because of him.

Las Vegas is actually where I first met Zeke. He was a grade higher in school than me but we lived in the same neighborhood and hung out. He had it rough like us and he always talked about getting out and becoming a tattoo artist and as soon as he was able to, he did just that. I always admired his determination and focus.

Me? Well, I never really knew what I wanted to do with

my life. I knew that I wanted to get out of Vegas and see more of the world but I had no idea career wise. I worked hard in high school and kept my grades up and then applied to every college on the east coast that I could find. I got accepted to the University of Pennsylvania and I can still remember the day I left for college. My mom had cried but I promised to fly her out to see me soon. I never wanted to return to Las Vegas and I haven't been back since.

College was a blur of late nights studying and weekends spent working at the campus bookstore and at a hardware store right off campus. It was hard to balance it all but worth it when I got my diplomas in business and restaurant management.

I kept in touch with Zeke even after he left and after I graduated and had opened up Lola, my first restaurant, I invited him out to see me. He was in California at the time but he came and ended up crashing on my couch for a week before he announced that he was sick of working for other people and that he was going to open his own place. I helped him find a place downtown and then became a silent partner in it. Then, when Zeke lost a bet to me, I got to name it and voila, Eye Candy Ink was born.

I love opening new places. I love fixing all of the little problems that pop up along the way. I love designing menus and figuring out the best location and ways to make each place stand out so that they become a success. I love the challenge of all of it but most of all, I just love controlling everything, having my decisions and planning be turned into a success.

Being a successful restaurateur hasn't left me with much time for dating or finding someone. I work long hours until the place is open and then I keep working, managing them after they're open. No one has ever tempted me before but something about Sam has me wanting to cut back on my hours.

I had wondered what she was going to do with that asshole who was hitting on her when I first got here. She was gorgeous, even with that bored out of her mind look on her face as she listened to him ramble on and on. I could tell that she wasn't interested in him and I had almost gotten up to help her get rid of him but something tells me that Sam doesn't like taking help from guys. She's more than capable of taking care of herself. She handled him like a champ and I wonder if that happens often. Maybe I could ask Zeke.

"How's the club coming along? Are you all ready for opening night?" Zeke asks as he takes a seat behind his desk.

"Yeah, I think so. I'm curious to see how it goes."

He rolls his eyes at that. "It will be great and you know it."

I grin at him, resting my foot on my knee as I lean back in my chair.

"So, what's the deal with Sam?"

Zeke's eyebrows rise so high that they almost touch his hair.

"When are you getting a haircut?" I ask before he can answer me and he flips me off.

"Chicks dig the long hair."

"How would you know that? You haven't been out on a date or with a woman in years, maybe even decades."

"Fuck you, it hasn't been that long."

"Yes it has!" A voice behind me says and I turn around, grinning when I see Mischa leaning against the doorframe.

He's wearing all black, that usual shit eating grin on his face and I stand up to hug him.

"Hey, Misch!" I say, pulling him into a hug before he can dart away.

"Get off of me," he says, but his tone is still playful. "I came here to mess with Zeke not to have you hanging all over me."

"I don't think you can make fun of anyone's relationship status, kid." I tell him, ruffling his hair before I head back to my chair.

"Actually, Mischa has a girlfriend now," Zeke says and he's grinning evilly at Mischa.

Mischa glares back at him as he plops down in the chair next to me.

"She's not my girlfriend," he mumbles and I raise my eyebrow at him.

"Mischa has a girlfriend. Has hell frozen over?"

He flips me off as Zeke and I laugh.

"Must be some girl. Does she have any friends for Zeke?"

"No, her friend is dating Atlas," Zeke says before Mischa can answer me.

"Good for him."

"Alright, I came back here to pick on Zeke and if that's not going to happen then I'm out. See you tomorrow, dad. Later, Uncle Max!"

Zeke and I both flip him off and he laughs and heads out the door.

"When are you going to fire that kid?"

"Don't talk about my son like that," Zeke deadpans.

"Right, let's talk about your sex life instead. Or lack thereof."

"I thought you wanted to talk about Sam?"

"Are you actually going to let me get to know her?" I ask. I saw how protective he was with her up front.

Zeke eyes me for a second before he nods. "I think you might be just what she needs."

"Then tell me about Sam." I say, leaning back in my chair again as he starts.

I hang on his every word and when we leave two hours later to head home, I have a pretty good idea of where to start to try to win the pretty, headstrong Samantha "Sam" Kavan over.

## 3

# S am

I SPIN AROUND in my office chair, my eyes staring at the ceiling as I slowly come to a stop. I sigh, stretching my arms overhead as the buzz of the tattoo machines and whatever music Mischa is currently blaring from his room fill the shop. I'm up front and we're technically closed but both Mischa and Nico's appointments ran over and Zeke is still finishing up payroll so I'm here waiting.

The guys don't like it when I walk alone to my car late at night and even though I'm only parked a block away, I kind of agree with them. Besides, it's not worth the lecture or worried texts and phone calls I'll get if I leave without one of them.

I'm about to do another spin when I hear Zeke's heavy boots making their way up front. *Finally.* He comes behind the front counter, shuffling some papers in his hands. He looks up and smiles at me before he tosses me an envelope with my paycheck in it.

"Thanks," I say, stuffing it into my bag underneath the counter.

He nods, putting the other envelopes in the trays underneath the whiteboard for Nico and Mischa to grab on their way out. Zeke sighs and rolls his shoulders as he leans against the back counter next to the shirts.

"Long night?" I ask, rocking side to side in my chair.

"Long week."

"You know I've heard that sex can help relieve stress," I say, teasing.

"Mischa?"

"Yep," I say, popping the p. "He was talking shit about how you can't get laid. He said it's been years," I say, drawing out the years and making Zeke chuckle.

"That boy," Zeke says but I can tell that he doesn't really care.

I laugh with him and soon I hear one of the tattoo machines turn off. *Almost time to head home.* I'm starving and I'm already wondering what I have to eat at home when Zeke interrupts my thoughts.

"Speaking of dating."

"Who was talking about dating?" I ask, confused.

"Max seemed taken with you."

I can't help but roll my eyes.

"He's a good guy," Zeke says and I nod my head.

I know that he and Zeke have been close for years, since they were just kids. Rumor has it that I have Max to thank for the Eye Candy Ink name and the bright pink logo. I've only heard of him in passing since he doesn't come to the shop all that often. I know from Zeke that he owns a few restaurants around town and that he grew up in Las Vegas too. Last night was the first time that I had met the guy though. I can see that he wasn't a dick. We actually had sort of a conversation and I didn't catch him staring at my tits or ass once. *Jesus, if that's how low my standards for guys to be good has gotten then something really has to change.*

"Yeah, he seemed alright."

"Whoa! I'm not sure the guy is ready for you to throw yourself at him like that."

I roll my eyes at Zeke as he grins.

"That's high praise coming from you," he continues.

"Whatever. I'm not interested in dating right now. My last, oh I don't know, five hundred, dates have been a freaking nightmare."

My phone buzzes on the counter and I spin around to see who could be messaging me.

**UNKNOWN:** Hey, it's Max. I'd love to take you out to dinner sometime.

MY STOMACH FLUTTERS when I see it's from Max and I do my best to repress that sensation. I *just* promised myself that I wouldn't date any more boys. *Max isn't a boy,* my subconscious whispers but I tell her to shut up. *Wait, how did he get my phone number?* I look over my shoulder, glaring at Zeke who gives me a sheepish smile.

"He's a good guy and I think you'd be good for each other."

I growl under my breath before I type out my response, ignoring the way my stomach twists and sinks.

.  .  .

**SAM:** No.

I SHOVE my phone in my bag before I can be tempted to take Max up on his offer and spin around to face Zeke. The other tattoo machine turns off and it's silent for a beat.

"I wish you'd give him a chance."

"What happens when things go bad? Whose side are you going to be on? How awkward is it going to be for me to work here?"

"Things won't go bad," he insists.

"You can't know that."

Voices come from down the hall and Mischa leads his two giggling girls up front. He looks like he's about to pull his hair out but he still gives them that grin that has girls going crazy. One steps up to hug him and he pulls back. I grin wider. I wonder if he knows just how far gone he is already for Indie. I check his client out and I want to point out that Indie hugs him but he heads back to clean up his room before I can.

"You think he knows he's in love with Indie yet?" I ask quietly after he disappears into his room.

"Hell no. He's going to fight his feelings for her tooth and nail. I just hope he doesn't fuck it all up before he realizes it."

Nico comes up then with the guy he had been working on and I cash him out and then lock the front door after him. I go back behind the desk to wait for Mischa and Nico to finish cleaning up. Zeke is still leaning against the back counter, watching me.

"What?"

"Speaking of people missing opportunities."

"Who was talking about that?"

"See you guys tomorrow!" Mischa calls as he practically sprints out of the shop.

"See you!" Zeke and I both call after him as we watch him go.

"Indie?" I ask.

"Yep," he says, popping the p and making me smile.

I can hear Nico moving around in his room and I know it won't be long now so I stand and pick up my bag, making sure that everything is in its place before I head out.

"I just want you to be happy, Sam," Zeke says from behind me and I nod my head, not turning around.

"I know, but I already am."

"I want you to be Mischa and Atlas happy."

"I think I'd need drugs or some kind of medication for that."

Zeke rolls his eyes, a smile playing on his lips as he lets the subject drop. I know that he cares about me, that all of the guys in the shop do, but I'm fine. I love my life and I don't need to be adding any more people to it.

Nico comes out then and we say goodbye to Zeke at the door as he leads me over to my car. He's tall and he towers over me. I watch his feet as we cross the parking lot to my old car.

"Hey, Nico?"

He stops and looks down at me.

"What do you think about Zeke's friend, Max?"

"Good guy," he says before he starts walking again.

"Marry him already, would ya," I tease and Nico smiles before he opens my car door for me.

"Night, Sam."

"See you tomorrow, Nico."

# 4

# M ax

I GROWL down at my phone when I check it for the hundredth time and see that Sam still hasn't responded to my latest message. I should be concentrating on work. I've been in my office in the back of Abernathy Brewhouse, staring at the same spreadsheet that I've been trying to figure out for the last hour and a half. This woman has me tied up in knots and I don't like it. I want to be the one tying her up in knots, in more ways than one.

Usually I'm good at reading people but I messed up with Sam. I shouldn't have invited her out to dinner so soon, but I was impatient. I've been out of the dating game for too long I guess. I jumped the gun. I take a deep breath. I need to get better at controlling myself where she's concerned. I don't want to blow it with her.

I've been trying to stop in and see her or text her a couple of times a week. I get the feeling that she doesn't take to people too quickly, so I need to get her used to me before I make my move. Nothing that I've done so far has seemed to help though.

I sent her two dozen red roses and she sent them back torn to shreds. I've brought her dinner and she's told me that she already ate. On nights that I can't go see her, I've had food delivered from some of the best restaurants in the city. She sent me back pictures of her eating crackers and chips from the vending machine. I try to text her most days and ask her about her day and she's brushed me off or ignored me.

I would have given up and left her alone a long time ago if not for the way I see her watching me when she thinks I'm not looking. I know that she can feel this thing between us too.

She's watching me right now. I can see her eyes roaming over me in the reflection on the front window. I'm up front catching up with Zeke but I've been keeping an eye on her the entire time that we've been talking.

I keep trying to remind myself that her generation is different from mine and they play these ridiculous games before they date or whatever the hell they call dating these days. I'm more than happy to chase Sam but I need to know that in the end, she wants to be caught by me. Otherwise, I'm no better than those other guys who hit on her and can't take a hint.

She acts differently with me than she does with them though. That guy the first night I met her, she couldn't wait to usher out the door. She had looked bored the entire time but she never looks bored around me. She might try to but there's always this spark in her eye and I can tell that she's interested in me too. Zeke even said that she asked about me one day.

Growing up poor taught me to fight and work hard for the things that I want and I want Sam. I'm a tenacious fucker by nature and I hate to lose. I hate losing even more when it's because I made a wrong move. Life is like a chess game. I made the wrong play when I first texted her and she took my pawn but I'm still in the game. I just need to tweak my strategy.

I've been trying to learn all that I can about her. I ask her a question every single day but I'm lucky if I get an answer. So far I've learned that she's twenty-five, a whole ten years younger than me, although that doesn't seem to bother either of us. That she refuses to date boys, or guys who act like little boys. She had looked me right in the eye when she told me that and I wanted to assure her that I was all man but a client had come in and she had to get back to work. I know that she has two older brothers who she assured me would murder me in my sleep if I got too close to her. She told me that one of them was a cop and knows how to get away with shit. I think she thought that would scare me off but I have a feeling that Sam is worth it.

I've noticed that she does that a lot. Gives people little tests. It's like she's seeing just how much someone cares about her, just how far they're willing to go. She's about to learn that I'll go all the way. That nothing can stop me from winning this game. I just need her to give me a shot.

For now, I'll keep coming by the shop and I'll keep trying with her. She's long term for me. I can just feel it.

## 5

---

# S am

I IGNORE the asshole who is trying to flirt with me at the bar. *Come on, bartender. Hurry it up so I can get the hell away from this guy.* I keep my eyes locked on the bartender as he makes up my drink, ducking out of the way when the guy talking to me almost smacks me in the face. *Who uses hand gestures like that in a crowded bar?* Someone who is so self-centered that they don't even realize there are other people around, that's who.

I finally get my drink and I toss a twenty on the bar, turning and walking away without a backward glance. I hear the guy call me a bitch and I just roll my eyes. What a prick.

I weave my way through the crowd, keeping a tight grip on the glass in my hand as I make my way toward where Mischa is waiting back by the speakers. My eyes look around, taking in the crowd around me as I finally get to where he's waiting for me.

"This place is filled with douchebags," I say as soon as I've made it back to where Mischa is hiding along the back wall. My eyes cut back to the asshole who had been trying to hit on me at the bar and I see he's already moved onto some other poor chick.

"Then why did you want to come here?" He asks, his tone bored.

"Just thought you should get out. You've been so gloomy these last few weeks. It's all anyone can talk about," I say sarcastically as I bring my whiskey sour to my lips and drink half of it in one big gulp.

"Great," he mumbles under his breath, taking another sip of his own beer.

He's been in a weird funk since he and Indie broke up. I can't believe I'm thinking this, but I miss the goofy guy that he was before. If only he would stop messing around and just admit that he likes her. *What, like you?* My subconscious asks. *That's not what I'm doing with Max. I just want to make sure that he really wants me before I potentially mess up my relationship with Zeke and have to find a new job.*

My subconscious rolls her eyes and I try not to think too much about why I chose to bring Mischa to Club Se7en. *Because it's Max's club and you wanted to see him.* My eyes scan the dark room, straining to see into each dark corner for his dark hair and sea green eyes.

"Who are you looking for?" Mischa asks and I jump. So much for me thinking that I was being discreet.

"No one," I say but the words come out rushed and I know without looking that Mischa can tell that I'm lying.

"Right," he drawls and I flip him off, bringing my glass to my lips and looking around one again.

Club Se7en just opened a couple of weeks ago and is already the hottest spot in the city. Max has been telling me that he'll put my name on the list for weeks and I think that I wanted to test that tonight and see if he really did. I'll admit, it was kind of cool being able to just breeze right inside instead of waiting in line with everyone else.

"Hey, you two," a deep voice says from my right and I jerk, biting back a sigh as Max emerges from a door next to us.

He smiles as he walks our way, his eyes raking over me and I try my best not to fidget as I shift closer to Mischa. Mischa holds his hand out to Max to shake and I watch as he reluctantly pulls his eyes away from me to say hello to him.

"Hey, man. Thanks for getting us in here," Mischa says but Max's eyes are already back on me and he's not paying Mischa any attention.

"Hello, Samantha."

"It's Sam, Max*WELL*," I snap back. I don't know why Max insists on calling me Samantha. Probably just to piss me off.

"You look beautiful," Max says, ignoring what I said and stepping closer to me.

"Yeah, when Mischa said he wanted to take me out tonight, I decided to dress up for him," I say, the lie coming easy. I smirk at Max, stepping into Mischa's side and wrapping my arm around his waist.

Mischa chokes on his sip of beer at my words and I want to laugh when I feel him tense ever more when Max shoots him a dirty look. I can tell that Mischa is going to tell him that I'm lying but before he can get the words out, a slinky blonde waitress comes up and taps Max on the shoulder. She whispers in his ear for a minute, pointing to the bar and he nods. I try to ignore the jealousy that courses through me when she touches him.

"If you'll excuse me, I have to see to a problem."

He looks right at Mischa when he says problem and I stifle another laugh. Mischa looks terrified and I can tell that he wants to tell Max that I'm full of shit so I lay my head against his shoulder and cuddle closer to Mischa. Max's glare intensifies and I'm pretty sure that he's about two seconds away from punching Mischa in the face when the blonde waitress tugs on his elbow again.

"I'll find you later," he says to me with a stern look.

"Don't bother. I'll be occupied."

A muscle in Max's jaw ticks as he turns and stalks away. I watch him go, my stomach sinking as he gets further away from me.

"Listen, Sam. I'm flattered, really, but I just don't see you like-"

"Oh, shut up!" I say as I hit Mischa in the arm. "I just needed him to think I was taken so that he would stop bothering me. I'm for sure not into you like that and everyone knows that you love Indie," I say, rolling her eyes.

"I'm not in love with Indie!" He growls, his voice coming out loud over the pounding music. "I don't do love. Anyone who says that they're in love is a dumb sucker who needs to see a physician about all of these delusions they're having. I am not, and will never, love someone."

A distressed gasp comes from behind him and I look over to see Indie standing there. She looks pale, like she was just slapped and part of me wants to slap Mischa for hurting her but we both stand frozen as she turns and bolts into the crowd.

"Way to go, asshole," I say but I'm not sure that Mischa

hears me. He's too busy staring at where Indie had disappeared.

We leave right after that. Mischa seems distracted and sad as he walks me out to my car and I keep glancing at him, trying to see if he's alright. He doesn't say anything as he closes my car door and I watch to make sure that he makes it to his car okay before I pull out of the lot.

I make it back to my apartment a few minutes later and walk up the stairs slowly. What am I doing? How can I judge Mischa for not admitting that he loves Indie when I can't even admit that I like Max. I keep pushing him away and then praying that he comes back. *What the hell is wrong with me?*

I'm just closing my apartment door behind me when a hand comes out and slams against the wood. I jerk back a step, eyes wide as the door swings open. Max stands there, his face tight as he looks past me into my apartment.

"Is he here?" He growls.

"Who?"

"Mischa."

"Oh, no. It's just me."

"So you were just teasing me? Do you want him?"

I shrug one shoulder. Nice to see that some of my attitude is coming back now that I know that I'm not about to be murdered.

"Enough, Samantha," Max almost growls as he backs me up against the wall. "I can't do these games anymore. I'm not some little boy that you can toy with. You say you don't want a boy, that you want a real man? Well sweetheart, I am a man and I want you. You want me to chase you? You want me to work for it? Sweetheart, I'm more than happy to do both but don't you ever pretend like you're with another man or interested in some other guy. Now you need to decide. Do you want me? If you don't then say it now and I swear I'll leave you alone."

"I don't want you," I say in a rush as my heart thunders in my ears. *Liar, liar, liar,* it says with each beat and I hold my breath. I don't want him to leave. I want him.

"Liar," he says as he cups my face in his hands. "Tell me the truth, Samantha."

"Fuck you, Maxwell," I say but it lacks my usual heat. Probably because he has me pinned between his hard body and the wall and I can feel everything through my thin jersey dress.

"I want to fuck you. I want you. All of you. Now tell me you want me too."

"Never."

"We'll see about that," he says as his hands tangle in my bright red hair and he angles my head back. His mouth hovers an inch above mine and I hold my breath, waiting for him to kiss me. I need him too. I need his lips on mine more than I need my next breath.

"I want you, Sam. But I'm not going to take you until you admit it too."

His lips brush the corner of my mouth and I bite back a groan at the soft caress.

"Don't take too long, Samantha. I'm not a patient man," he says before he turns and heads back out the door, leaving me a panting, shaking, horny mess.

# 6

# Max

I'VE ALWAYS BEEN good at reading people and situations. It's how I've gotten so far in life and business. I'm willing to gamble on my gut. Which is exactly what I did that night with Sam.

I had almost lost it when she had wrapped her arm around Mischa. I love that kid but I'm not messing around when it comes to Sam being mine. I had watched them leave together and I had followed them, letting out a breath when I saw them leave in separate cars. I still had to follow her home. I told myself it was to make sure that she got there alright, but really I wanted to make sure that she wasn't meeting him back at her place.

She's feisty and strong willed and I know that she was fighting this thing between us but I don't think that she'll be able to resist a challenge.

Or I didn't.

Now, I'm starting to have doubts. It's been three weeks now since that night I laid down my challenge and told her to come find me when she made up her mind about us. I haven't heard from her since that night either. I thought if I gave her space that she would realize how much she liked having me around and miss me. Now I'm wondering if I really know a damn thing about women or this particular one.

She's the only woman who matters. I know I promised that I would leave her alone if she didn't want me too but thinking about not seeing her again has a lead weight settling in my stomach. It feels like someone is trying to pull my heart out. Like I'm not whole without her in my life. When the fuck did that happen?

All of this has led to a lot of confusion and stress over the last few weeks. Maybe that's why I haven't been in the best mood. I'm at Abernathy Brewhouse, filling in for my head chef who just quit and walked out. He thinks that he's too good to be working in a pub. He's about to find out that my connections are wide and no one that I know will touch him with a ten-foot pole. I'm looking to turn him away when he comes crawling back but for now, I need to figure out the menu and get everything running smoothly again.

The kitchen is chaotic since we're in the middle of the dinner rush and I'm sweating from the heat of the ovens and stoves, bent over the counter as I try to arrange the truffle burger on the little tray just right. Dress pants and a button-down shirt are not the things to be wearing in this environment and I let out a puff of breath, dying to go outside for just a second to cool down. Servers bustle pass me, asking for orders and taking out trays but I ignore it. I've almost got this tray just right when the kitchen door bursts open and I jerk, sending fries skittering across the counter and onto the floor. I curse under my breath, standing up as my patience snaps.

"For fucks sake! What? What do you want?" I snap, spinning on my heels to face the person who just barged into my kitchen.

Sam stands there in a pair of frayed blue jeans and a black Eye Candy Ink shirt. She must have come to see me on her break. Her eyes are wide as she looks around the mess that is the Abernathy Brewhouse kitchen. I rub my own eyes, exhausted from this whole day, from the last three weeks.

"I don't have time for this," I murmur under my breath but when I open my eyes, I can tell that Sam heard me. Regret fills me and I want to snatch the words back. I step forward but she takes a step back.

"You can't be in here, Samantha. If the health inspector saw you in here, he would shut me down." I try to soften my words but she still looks taken aback and pissed off as she turns to leave and I know that I just royally fucked up.

"Fuck."

The kitchen is silent as the door swings shut and I know that I should say something to the staff to get back to work but I don't have it in me. The bitter taste of the words I just said to Sam are still in my mouth and I just want to go home and crawl into bed and forget this day ever happened but I know that I can't.

I know that Sam won't forget either and I'm already anticipating her making me pay for this. I deserve it, but after this shitty week, all I want is to talk to her. Too bad I just messed that up.

# 7

S am

"HE DOESN'T HAVE time for me? Who the hell does he think he is? I finally give in and go see him and then he yells at me and treats me like I'm some whiny kid who's underfoot? Hell. No," I keep mumbling to myself as I hammer away at the computer keyboard, typing in the next client's info. The girl in front of me looks terrified and I try to smile at her but that doesn't seem to help.

I realize that I look crazy, mumbling to myself with a pissed off expression on my face but I *AM* pissed off. How dare Max treat me like that. Fuck him. This just shows that you really have to choose your person wisely. I almost gave into Max and look at how quickly he turned. Hurt slices through me when I remember the way he had talked to me at the brewhouse and I wince, pushing those thoughts away.

It's easier to feel pissed than hurt, so I've been trying all week to stay mad.

I think I would have written him off by now but something is holding me back. In his defense, he has been trying to apologize all week. He's sent flowers, chocolates, and food to the shop every single night with little notes but I just throw it all away. I've been ignoring his calls and texts too. I'm expecting him to show up at the shop any day now. I'm actually surprised that he hasn't but I have a feeling that Zeke told him to stay away. I didn't tell him what happened but he knows that I came to work upset and that Max has something to do with it.

As if my thoughts have conjured him, the front door opens and there he is. His eyes are locked on me and I narrow mine as I meet their bright green gaze. He comes to a stop a few feet from the front counter and I continue to glare at him.

"I'm sorry."

My eyes cut away from him and I notice the girl I just checked in is riveted to the scene in front of her.

"Not good enough."

"Let me take you out."

"Fuck. No."

"Alright. Not tonight then. What about tomorrow?"

"Can't, I have plans."

"Doing what?"

"I need to dye my hair," I say, twirling a few strands around my finger as I try to look as bored as possible.

"I can help you with that."

"Hard pass."

"Samantha, I'm sorry," he says and for the first time, I notice just how tired he looks. There are dark circles under his eyes and his hair is mussed. His shirt is wrinkled and his jeans look like he might have slept in them. As I look him over, I can feel myself softening and I straighten my shoulders, steeling myself against that and holding onto my anger.

"I don't forgive you. I'm a fucking lady and no one is allowed to talk to me that way."

"I know. I'm so sorry and I swear that it will never happen again. How can I prove that? How can I make it up to you?"

He steps closer to the counter, his eyes pleading and an evil thought enters my mind.

"Let me pierce you."

"Alright," he answers right away and I try not to let the shock show on my face.

He's got to be bluffing. Or maybe he thinks I'm going to pierce his ear or something. I wasn't really clear but part of me wants to test him, to see how far he's really willing to go for me.

"Hey, Nico?"

A second later, I hear Nico moving around in his room and then he pokes his head out.

"Can you watch the counter for a bit? I have a client," I say, nodding my head towards Max.

Nico's eyebrows raise but he just nods and comes out to take over for me.

"Right this way, Maxwell," I say in my sweetest voice, opening the gate and leading him down the short hallway to my room.

# 8

---

# M<sup>ax</sup>

I FOLLOW BEHIND SAM, trying not to show just how nervous I am. I have a feeling that she can smell fear and I want to show her that I'm sure about us and that I would do anything for her. She leads me into a room painted a royal shade of purple with some antique looking light fixture hanging from the ceiling. There's a long chair in the middle of the room with posters of piercing placements on the walls. She heads right over to her desk on the far wall and pulls out some gloves and other equipment.

I'm okay with tattoos but I've never thought about piercing something. As I look around at the posters of different types of piercings and then back to the pissed off look on Sam's face, I start to have second thoughts.

"What kind of piercing did you want?" She asks but it feels like another one of her tests.

"Whatever you want."

"The apadravya then."

The idea of her pissed off, shoving a needle through my dick has me sweating but if it gets her to forgive me then a little pain will be worth it. *I hope.*

"Take your pants off and sit right here," she says, patting the chair with a terrifying smile.

I watch her pull out a few things and line them up on the desk. Her movements are confident and sure and I love seeing her like this. So in her element. Then I remember what's about to happen and I'm back to feeling nauseous.

I pull my pants and boxers off slowly, setting them on the chair next to her desk before I sit down gingerly on the table. I watch her face as she turns and looks at my cock for the first time but she gives nothing away.

"Now, you won't be able to have sex for at least three months after this. Or however long it takes for the piercing to heal. Still want to do this?"

*Another test.*

"Three months, huh?"

"If you want to sleep with me, it will be at least three months before you get laid."

I study her face and I can feel it. This is a big moment for us. She needs to see that I want her, no matter what. That I'll wait for her and be stable and supportive.

"I can wait," I say quietly as I stare into her eyes and she swallows hard before she turns around and snaps on some latex gloves.

I try to block out what happens next. All I remember is some ice and then a stabbing pain followed by a lot of swearing from me. When the worst of the pain is over, I look up to see Sam has already cleaned up and is just sitting there smiling at me like the Cheshire Cat.

"I think you might be a little sadistic," I say as she passes me my clothes and I start to pull them on.

"Maybe, but you're the one chasing me. I wonder what that says about you?"

I stand up, buttoning my jeans as she pushes her desk chair back in and starts to brush past me. Before she can escape, I'm on her.

I crowd into her space, backing her against the wall and pinning her hands to the wall above her head.

"I'm sorry. I'm so fucking sorry. I was having a really shitty day and I took it out on you. I like things to be ordered and running smoothly."

"You like to be in control," she interrupts me and I nod admitting that point.

"I do. The kitchen was in chaos and the staff was falling apart and then you burst in and I took all of my frustrations out on you and I'm sorry. I regretted it as soon as I said it. As soon as the words left my lips, I wanted to take them back. I never should have spoken to you like that and I swear, I never will again."

"No one speaks to me that way," she says, her chin tipping up. She looks down her nose at me, like a queen assessing some peasant and I think I fall in love with her right then and there.

Even with me holding her hands imprisoned above her head, she still doesn't back down. She doesn't show an ounce of vulnerability or mercy. Sam is tough and strong and she might look like a queen right now but I know that she would hate it if I treated her like one.

She doesn't want a man who puts her on a pedestal. She would be bored out of her mind if I did. She doesn't want a man who is going to treat her like she's made of glass. She wants a man, a real man, who is going to be her partner.

Someone who will have her back and support her without smothering her. I aim to be that man.

"I'm sorry. I swear it will never happen again."

She eyes me, but she must see that I'm sincere because she relaxes in my hold and nods slightly. I reluctantly release her hands and step back slightly.

"Am I forgiven?"

"Yeah," she says before she stands on her tiptoes and brushes a feather soft kiss against my lips.

"That will be fifty dollars plus tip," she says over her shoulder as she opens the door and heads back up front.

I can't fight the smile that stretches my lips as I watch her go. This girl has got me by the balls but I don't mind one bit.

# 9

# Sam

I BITE BACK a smile the next night when I see Max heading for the front door. I was wondering when he would be back and I'm pleased that it didn't take him long. It's almost closing time and I figured he wouldn't be in tonight but here he is.

He reaches for the front door handle and I notice the paper bags he's carrying in his other hand. I pretend not to see him as I get busy organizing my desk and packing up my bag for the night. Atlas is still here with a client but Zeke said he'd stay until they were done. I was going to wait until one of them could walk me to my car but now that Max is here, I'll just have him do it instead.

I slip my bag onto my shoulder as he comes in and walks up to the front counter.

"Samantha," he says and I bite back a smile. I kind of

like how he never bothers with the pleasantries with me. It's always just my name whenever he sees me, like he's forgotten that other words exist.

"Hey," I say, meeting his eyes.

"Are you heading home?"

"Yeah, I was just about to leave. Walk me to my car?"

"Of course."

I smile at him before I head for the gate, calling over my shoulder to Zeke and Atlas before I open it.

"I'll see you tomorrow!"

"Wait!" Zeke calls and I look back to see that both Atlas and Zeke have poked their heads out of their rooms.

"I'll walk you to your car," Zeke says at the same time that Atlas asks me who is walking me to my car.

"That's okay. Max said he'll do it."

Atlas's eyebrows shoot up but Zeke just grins at me.

"Have fun, kids," he says with a knowing tone before he heads back into his office.

Atlas looks confused for a second, looking between me and where Zeke disappeared.

"Okay... Night, Sam."

"Night, Atty!"

I let the gate bang closed behind me before I lead Max out the front door. We turn left and walk down the sidewalk side by side until we reach the parking lot next to the shop.

"So, are you going to tell me what's in the bags?" I ask.

He waits until we reach my car before he sets the bags on the ground and pulls out what's inside. He hands me a black box first with Converse written on it and I smile when I open the lid to see a pair of neon pink high tops inside. He passes me another box before I can say anything and I laugh when I see the matching pink hair dye.

"I thought we could eat dinner and dye your hair," he

says, waving the other bag at me and my stomach growls when I think about food.

I tap my chin, pretending to think about it and he steps into me, pinning me against my car door.

"Please, Samantha."

"Alright," I relent, reaching for my car door when he smiles at me. "You can meet me at my place."

He nods, waiting until I'm inside my car with it started before he heads over to his. I see that it's parked close by and I wait until he's in before I pull out of the lot and make the short drive home. The whole way home I'm wondering how messy my apartment is. I've been working the last four days so I haven't had much time to pick up or do chores. Maybe I can rush inside and upstairs before he gets here.

That thought was dashed when I park and look up to see Max already walking my way. *How the hell did he find a parking spot so fast?* He opens my door for me and I slide out.

"Thanks," I say as I grab the bag with the shoes and hair dye.

He nods, taking the bag from me as I lead us inside the building and up to my apartment.

"It might be a little bit of a mess," I warn as I unlock the door.

"I don't mind messy."

Something about the way he says it has me pausing. It sounds like he's talking about more than my apartment and my heart clenches as I bite back a grin. I push the door open and usher him inside.

My place is nothing fancy. A studio apartment closer to the outskirts than downtown but it's close to work and was all that I could afford if I didn't want to have three room-mates. Everything is out in the open except the bathroom and I wince when I see the dirty dishes piled in the sink and my hamper in the corner overflowing with clothes.

"I expected more color," Max says as he turns in a circle in the center of the space.

"More color?"

"Yeah, on the walls and stuff. Everything is white and black. It kind of looks like my place."

"Paint is expensive and I'm not here all that much. Maybe if I owned my own place I would paint and decorate more but I rent this."

I look around, trying to see what he sees. The walls are all an off-white color and I never got around to hanging anything up so they're all bare. My futon is black and off to one side, pulled out since I never bother making it. I have one end table next to that that's also black and serves as a little kitchen table as well. The appliances in the kitchen are all white. The only color besides that is the carpet which is brown and I'm not sure if that really counts as color.

"Eat first?" He asks, holding up the brown paper bag.

"Sure," I say, heading past him to grab two plates from the cabinet and some silverware.

He's pulled everything out and set it on the little kitchen island and I pass him one of the plates and a fork before I start lifting the lids off the containers.

"Burgers and fries okay?" He asks and my stomach growls.

He grins and I nod, biting into my burger. We eat standing up at the little island. My kitchen light bulb burned out the other day so the only light is from the lamp in the living room. I suddenly feel self conscious. Max is some super successful dude. Is he going to take one look at all of this and never call me again?

I set the french fry I had been about to eat down and

push my takeout container away from me, suddenly losing my appetite. When I look up, Max is watching me with a thoughtful look on his face.

"What?" I snap.

He smiles softly.

"I'm just waiting for the next test."

"What? What test?"

"That's how you get to trust people. You give them little tests. If they don't pass, then you write them off as someone who doesn't care about you in the long run."

"No, I don't," I insist, my stomach tightening.

*Do I really do that?*

"You did it with Mischa at the club, wanting to see if I would fight for you. The piercing yesterday? To see if I was willing to go through whatever for you. I promise you, Samantha. I'm here for the long haul. I'd do anything for you."

"Even live here? With my one lightbulb and sink full of dirty dishes?"

"Are you asking me to move in with you?" The excitement and hope in his eyes doesn't go unnoticed by me and I shift.

"No, this is another test."

"Yeah, Samantha. I'd live anywhere with you. I don't care about the surroundings. Just that you're there with me."

My heart melts at his words and the sincerity that I see in his eyes and I hurry to avert my eyes. I clear my throat, taking a deep breath before my eyes snag on the Converse and hair dye on the counter.

"Ready to help me dye my hair?"

"Sure, although I don't know how much help I'll be."

He picks one of the boxes up and examines it, reading the instructions. I grab my old towel and change into a paint stained tank top before I come back out to the kitchen. We spend the next ten minutes spreading the dye onto my hair and combing it through to make sure it gets to each strand. I put the shower cap on after and lean against the counter.

He eyes my hair and then his gloves before he meets my eyes.

"Now what?"

"Now we wait a bit and then wash it out."

He nods, pulling his gloves off.

"I think I'm going to be an expert at this in no time."

"You think you'll be around in a few weeks to help me again?"

"Yeah, I do."

We stare at each other in silence for a beat and I can feel myself warming to him even more.

"So, what started this?" He asks, waving his hand to my head and then to the new Converse on the counter.

"I just liked dying my hair. I had it pink the first time I dyed it and it was awesome. It looked like my hair was cotton candy. I rocked it for a bit but the pastels faded really fast so then I just dyed it again. It was navy blue the second time and I just never really stopped. I have to buy the good stuff so that I don't fry my hair but I love switching it up every few weeks."

"Did I get the right stuff? I asked the saleslady and she said that brand was good but I didn't know anything about it."

"Yeah. You actually got the really good stuff. Thanks, by the way."

"Anytime, Samantha."

"Why do you always call me that?"

"It's your name."

"Yeah, but everyone calls me Sam. You're the only one who calls me Samantha."

"I guess Sam sounds like a buddy's name to me and I want to be way more than your buddy. Do you not like Samantha?"

I never have before but when it comes from his mouth, my name sounds beautiful.

"No, it's fine."

"Beautiful name for a beautiful girl."

"Oh man! I think that was the cheesiest thing that I've ever heard," I say, laughing as I lean back against the kitchen island.

Max gives me a sheepish smile but it grows when he sees me laughing.

"It's true."

"Bleh!"

That makes him laugh and soon we're standing in my dimly lit apartment, laughing like lunatics. The city has grown quiet outside my apartment and it kind of feels like we're the only two people alive.

My alarm goes off and our moment is broken. I shut off the alarm and head to the sink, pulling the shower cap off as I bend over. Max moves behind me and I feel him brush against my ass as he leans over me to grab the sink sprayer. He turns it on, testing the water before he starts to slowly wash out my hair. I watch the pink dye swirl down the drain until the water runs clear. Max shuts the faucet off and I stand up, wrapping the towel around my wet hair.

When I stand up, he's right there and I can't wait any longer. I'm sick of the games, of testing him and seeing if he'll pass. I have a feeling that Max will pass anything that I can throw his way. I want him and I'm done fighting this feeling.

I step toward him, tipping my face up towards his and licking my lips. His eyes flare, turning a darker blue as he leans toward me. *Yes!* My mind screams as I feel his warm breath fan over my face. Anticipation floods my bloodstream and I raise up onto my tiptoes, wanting his mouth on mine already.

I expected that the first time that Max kissed me would be hard and fast. Most guys when you give them the green light can't wait to get down to business but not Max. He takes his time backing me up until I pressed against the wall. He reaches up and brushes a stray lock of hair back behind my ear before his hand caresses my cheek. His eyes study my face like he's trying to brand it to his memory and by the time his thumb traces my bottom lip, I'm panting and on the verge of begging him to kiss me. It feels like if I don't find out what his lips taste and feel like in the next five seconds, I'll die.

Finally, his lips press against mine and it's even better than I could have imagined. His mouth moves skillfully against mine, his movements almost lazy as we learn the shape and taste and texture of each other. His lips open and his tongue licks against my lower lip, begging for entry. I open, greedy for his taste. Things speed up after that and he lifts me onto the kitchen counter next to the sink, spreading my legs wide so he can fit between them. I wrap my arms around his neck, threading my fingers into my hair and he groans into my mouth.

He grips my hips, dragging me to the edge of the counter and grinds against me. I gasp into his mouth when I feel his hard length pressing against me. I rock against him and I swear I'm close to coming when he swears and jerks away from me.

"Shit," he swears, doubling over.

"Oh my god, are you okay?" I ask, hopping off the counter and going over to him.

The towel has come loose from my hair and I toss it onto the ground as I bend over next to him.

"What's wrong?"

"The piercing," he grits out.

"The pier-OH!"

"It got caught on my jeans," he says as he stands up and hobbles over to the futon.

"Yeah, it might take you some time to get used to it."

I grab him some ice and wrap it in a kitchen towel before I clean up the kitchen and go over to the futon. I stretch out alongside him and he blinks his eyes open, turning to look at me.

"Sleep here," I say and he just smiles, setting the ice aside and pulling me into his arms.

I fall asleep that night with my head on his chest, listening to his steady heartbeat as I drift of to sleep.

# 10

# M ax

I PULL up outside Eye Candy Ink and shift into park. Before I can unbuckle my seatbelt, the passenger and rear door open and Atlas and Mischa slide inside.

"Hey, guys," I say, eyeing them warily as they get settled in the seats.

The shop hasn't opened yet and I was hoping to surprise Sam with some breakfast. I haven't seen her all week since I'm still struggling to find a new chef for Abernathy Brewhouse. I've had to spend my nights there and it's been killing me. I have a couple people interviewing today and hopefully I can hire someone and then get back to seeing Sam at night. I miss dropping in with dinner or taking her out for a quick bite to eat on her break.

"What's up?" I ask when they haven't said anything.

Mischa opens his mouth but before he can, the back door opens again and Zeke slides in next to Atlas.

"What are we doing?"

"I don't know," I say, turning in the driver's seat to look at him.

"We're getting to that!" Mischa says, rolling his eyes.

"Okay, so spit it-oh, what the hell!"

I don't know if I should laugh or curse when the door opens again and Nico climbs in next to Zeke. My car was not built for five grown men and it's funny to see Zeke smashed between Nico and Atlas in the back while Mischa, the skinniest of all of us, is comfortable in the front seat.

"I think Mischa should trade seats with me," Zeke says and I do laugh then.

"Why are we all in my car?"

"We needed to talk to you," Atlas says from behind me.

"In private," Mischa adds, looking around like he's a super-secret spy before he slinks down in his seat.

"Okay," I say, drawing out the word. "About what?"

"Sam," Atlas says.

"Yeah, what are your intentions with her?" Mischa asks, crossing his arms and trying to look stern but he can't really pull it off when he's also hunched down in the seat.

"Shouldn't *I* be asking that question?" Zeke asks from the back.

"No, her real dad and brothers should," Nico adds in his usual no nonsense tone.

"Excuse me!?! *REAL* brothers and dad? What the heck are we?" Mischa asks, turning in his seat to glare at Nico in the back.

Nico grins at Mischa and I think it's the first time that I've seen the guy smile.

"I think Sam seems happy. I don't know why we're here," Atlas pipes in and Mischa turns his glare on him.

"It's our job! We have to know that Max is a good guy and that he's going to treat her right."

"But we know Max and he is a good guy and he is treating her right," Nico points out and Mischa throws his hands in the air, rolling his eyes again.

Zeke is grinning like a lunatic in the backseat and I honestly don't know how to respond.

"I'm not going to hurt, Sam. I love her. I would never... I never want to do anything to hurt her," I say quietly and the car falls silent.

Everyone seems to be weighing my words, trying to decide if I'm being sincere or not, but I am and after a minute, the energy changes and it's light and carefree between us all once more.

"How's Indie?" I ask Mischa.

Sam told me that they were trying to work things out but I hadn't heard anything since. Mischa's whole mood changes as soon as her name is brought up. His eyes get softer and he has a smile playing around his lips. I wonder if I look like that when I think about Sam. Oh, who am I kidding, of course I do.

"She's good," he says and I notice Zeke grinning wider.

"That's my boy," he says, reaching forward and clapping Mischa on the shoulder.

"Oh my god, dad. You're embarrassing me," he mumbles but I see that he's smiling.

"What about you, Atlas? How's your girl?" I ask, turning to look at him in the back.

"She's great. I'm actually... I'm going to ask her to marry me," he says quietly.

The car explodes with sounds of congratulations and

Mischa practically climbs into the backseat to hug him. I laugh at his antics but Nico and Zeke are also trying to hug him and it just looks like a pile of bodies. I laugh, turning in my seat and that's when I see her.

Sam is standing outside the car, a bewildered expression on her face as she tries to comprehend what is happening inside the car. I wave at her, smiling wider, and she returns it, stepping around the hood and to my door. I open it and drag her into my lap, slamming the door closed behind us.

"What are you all doing?" She asks, her hand wrapping around my shoulder as she tries to peer into the backseat.

Mischa is still halfway in the backseat and we have to help drag him back into the front. Sam laughs when his elbow bounces off the roof and he swears and I smile, loving the sound of her laugh, of her happy.

"I think your friends are crazy," I tell Sam.

"Hey! We're your friends too," Zeke says from the backseat and I just shake my head.

Yeah, I guess he's right.

"What are we doing here?" Sam asks, leaning back against the door.

"I came to bring you breakfast. They all just climbed in," I tell her.

"Atlas is getting married!" Mischa shouts and Sam blinks for a second before she grabs the seat lever and lowers the driver's seat into Atlas's lap.

She climbs over me and hugs him and I just grin as everyone complains.

"Congratulations!" She tells him as I raise the seat back upright and she settles back into me.

"She hasn't said yes yet," he says, playing with his fingers in his lap.

"She will," everyone says in unison.

"Well, we better get inside," Zeke says clapping his hands.

They all clamber out of the car, waving goodbye to me. Mischa snags the takeout bag off the floor of the passenger seat and then bolts inside. Sam laughs and chases after him and I smile when I see Atlas and Nico just shake their heads and follow them inside. Zeke is the last one to leave and he watches me from the backseat.

"I don't think we have anything to be worried about," he says quietly, before he nods his head at me and follows them inside.

My phone buzzes in my cup holder and I pick it up, smiling when I see Samantha on the screen.

**SAMANTHA:** Sorry about breakfast. How about you take me out to dinner tomorrow?"

**MAX:** It's a date.

THAT DIDN'T GO the way I had planned but I got Sam's surrogate family's approval and another date with her so it's still a win in my book. I drive to work with a smile on my face.

## 11

----

# S am

I SMILE when Max gets my door for me. He's always doing that and it's weird because no one ever has for me before. He also sends me flowers every week and he's always stopping by with food and snacks. Last week he came by my apartment and changed my burnt-out lightbulb for me. We had made out on my futon for half an hour after that and my lips had tingled for hours after he left.

He stops in to see me when he can and we text and talk on the phone every day. I never realized how strange my hours are until I started dating him. Since we both work more at night, we end up hanging out more in the mornings. We try to grab breakfast or coffee together a few times a week but it's not the same as an actual nighttime date with him.

I think he must have felt the same because when I told him I had this Thursday off, he had immediately changed his meeting to a different day and told me that he would pick me up at seven. I dressed up for him, wearing the only nice thing I own, a tight black halter dress and a pair of black high heels. All of my tattoos are on display and my hair is still dyed a bright pink color. Max mentioned that he ran to the store this morning and I'm dying to see which color hair dye he picked out for me now. I saw the bag and the Converse box in the backseat already but he didn't bring it up so I decided to wait.

We're at some fancy new restaurant that opened up downtown a few months ago. I've heard that it's almost impossible to get reservations but I guess not when you have connections like Max does.

He holds the door open for me and I smile at him as I pass inside. This place is crazy. It's all tall ceilings and glass windows. A glass staircase leads up to the second floor and there are tables scattered throughout so that the effect is intimate and classy. I can see people giving me weird looks already as Max and I follow after the hostess to our table in the corner. He pulls my chair out for me and I murmur a thank you as I drop down into it and reach for my menu.

"This place is beautiful. Is it one of yours?" I ask when he takes his seat.

"No, I thought it seemed tacky to take you out to one of my restaurants on our first date."

"Is this our first date?"

"First official date, I guess? Are you counting all of the breakfast dates or when I bring dinner to the shop?" He asks as he picks up his own menu but I notice that he doesn't open it. Instead, his eyes stay locked on me.

"I wasn't sure what to count. It's just that after three dates, I typically go past first base."

His eyes heat and I smirk at him over the top of my menu.

"I'm counting every time we've eaten together then."

I laugh at that and notice a few people turn our way and shoot me dirty looks.

"Does it bother you?" I ask him, nodding to the people staring at us.

"What?" Max asks and I see that he hasn't taken his eyes off me.

"People staring at us like that. Like you should be with someone more... normal."

"I don't care what anyone thinks. I want you, Samantha. Only you."

I smile shyly at that. "So, you like all of my tattoos and piercings then?"

"I fucking love them. Although I don't think that I've seen all of them yet," he says, his eyes heating as he looks over my body.

"You haven't," I say, my voice coming out husky.

Before he can respond, the waiter comes over and asks us what we'd like to drink. I let Max talk wines with him and order for both of us as I look over the menu. It's an upscale seafood place but I don't really like fish and I'm allergic to shellfish. I try to find a different option but it doesn't look like there is any.

"What looks good?" Max asks as he opens his own menu.

"This salted caramel cheesecake."

He laughs at that and I smile, loving the sound.

"We can get dessert. What did you want as a main course though?"

"Um..." I trail off, looking over the small menu for some option that I might have missed.

"Are you not hungry?"

"I'm allergic to shellfish," I admit.

"Shit, I'm so sorry, Samantha. I should have asked before I made reservations. Let's go. We can find someplace else," he says as he drops his napkin and a hundred on the table and stands up.

He pulls my chair out for me and links our hands together as he drags me out of the restaurant.

"Are you going to be okay? I mean you breathed it in. How does that work?" He asks as he tucks me into his car. I smile, loving how concerned he is about me.

"I have to eat it. I'll be fine."

He nods and climbs behind the wheel.

"What would you like to eat?" He asks as he starts the car.

We're in downtown so there's a lot of choices but it's late and without reservations, we can't really go anywhere fancy.

"There's this crappy little Chinese restaurant by my place," I say, leaning over the center console and placing my hand on his thigh.

Max shifts, cupping my face in his hands and kissing me. His mouth moves over mine, hungry and I moan when he nips my bottom lip. I love the way this man kisses me. Like he can't get enough. Like he's afraid that I'll pull away or be taken from him at any moment. Like he can't breathe without me.

A car horn honks nearby and we both pull apart reluctantly.

"So Chinese?" He asks.

"Yeah. Then dessert."

I order the food while Max drives. He runs in and grabs

it as soon as we pull up and I smile at his eagerness. Before I know it, we're pulling up in front of my place. Max grabs the food and comes around to the passenger side, grabbing my hand and tugging me after him up the steps. I laugh, picking up my pace to keep up with him.

We tumble into my apartment, both of us breathless and grinning like loons at each other. We come up short when I notice my brothers and dad sitting on my futon. They put it up and are all staring wide eyed at us.

Max stiffens next to me, fixing his dress shirt that I somehow managed to undo two buttons on. I straighten my dress too, my face flaming red as I look anywhere but at them.

"Hey, guys. What are you doing here?" I ask as I step further into the room.

"We all had tomorrow off so we came to surprise you," my dad says.

"Who the hell is this?" Both my brothers ask in unison.

"Hi, I'm Max," Max says as he steps past me and holds his hand out to my dad first and then my brothers.

They all hesitate but eventually they shake hands with him. I see him shaking out his fingers when he pulls away from my older brother Miles. He's got his cop face on and I can tell that he's gearing up to interrogate Max. Abe is sitting next to him, eyeing him like he thinks Max might be a threat. The only one who doesn't look like he wants to murder Max is my dad, who is sitting on the end, watching Max with a speculative look on his face.

"Where did you two meet?" Miles asks and I roll my eyes as the interrogation begins.

"At work."

"How long have you been seeing each other?" He asks as he crosses his arms over his chest and glares at Max.

"A couple of months," he says back calmly.

*Has it really been that long already?*

"Hm. Why didn't you tell us about him?" Miles asks, turning his stare on me.

"I was trying to avoid this," I say, twirling a finger around my small apartment.

"Is he treating you right?" Abe asks, like Max isn't standing right there.

"Of course! You think I would be with a guy who didn't treat me right? You all taught me better than that."

They all seem to relax a little after I say that. I know that they care about me and just want the best for me but this is a little ridiculous.

"What do you do for a living, Max?" My dad asks, leaning back against the futon.

"I'm a restauranteur."

Max moves over to the kitchen island, setting the food down before he turns to face them.

"You own restaurants and yet you're getting my baby sister takeout?" Miles asks.

"We were at this other restaurant but it was seafood and I didn't know that she was allergic. So we left and got Chinese."

"And the Chinese takeout was my idea," I say before they can ask him anything else.

I give them all a hard look and they eye me back.

"Why don't you give us a minute alone with Max?" My dad asks but it's not really a question.

"I forgot your hair dye and shoes in the car," Max says, handing me his keys.

He kisses me quickly and with one last warning glance back at my family, I head down the stairs and out front to

Max's car. He's parked right by the front door and I hurry to grab the box out of the back before I rush back upstairs.

When I get there, everyone looks more relaxed and I eye all of them suspiciously.

"Well, we're going to get going. We'll see you both soon," my dad says before he comes over and hugs me.

Miles and Abe follow his lead, giving me a hug and in Abe's case, a noogie, before they file out the door and down the stairs.

My apartment is silent after the door closes and I turn to watch Max. He doesn't look scared or like he's ready to bolt for the door. I relax when he smiles at me softly.

"So, that was my family," I say, turning to see how Max is dealing with us being ambushed like that.

"I like them," he says with a smile.

"Really?"

"Yeah. It's obvious that they love you and want you to be taken care of. I promise, I'm going to take care of you. And I love you," he says as he wraps his arms around my waist and tugs me into him.

"Okay, one. I can take care of myself."

"I know you can," he says before I can get mad. "But you don't have to do everything by yourself. You don't have to be tough all of the time around me, Sam."

"You called me Sam."

I don't know why but I kind of miss him calling me Samantha.

"Just this once."

I roll my eyes.

"What was number two?"

I bite my bottom lip. Is it too soon to say this? We've only been together a couple of weeks really. *But you've known each other for months. He's been showing you that he wants you, that he wants to be there for you for months. You trust him. You want him. You love him.*

"I love you too," I finally spit out.

Max's face almost splits in two when he smiles down at me and the next thing I know, he's pulling the futon out and laying me down on it. His lips meet mine and I'm lost in him. It feels different now that we've both said the L word. Bigger and deeper somehow. Soon, I'm lost in him and it's hard to tell where he ends and I begin. He's stripped me naked and lays me back down on the futon and I expect him to come down over me but instead, he kisses across my belly and down to my mound. I shift, spreading my legs wider as he settles between them.

"I like your piercings," he murmurs against my skin and I smile.

He hadn't said anything about the nipple piercings the first time he saw them but going by the way his eyes had widened and how enthusiastic he had been to play with them, I knew that he liked those. I didn't tell him about my clitoral hood piercing though.

His fingers form a V and he spreads my lower lips, admiring the jewelry nestled between my folds. I moan when he leans forward and licks a straight path up my center, his tongue nudging my clit at the end.

"I *love* your piercings," he mumbles before we both stop talking.

He licks and nips along my folds, dipping into my hole before he licks back up to my clit. His fingers play with the piercing, snaking up my body to give my nipples some attention too. I've never been that loud during sex, but with Max, I can't seem to help myself. He rubs my clit as his tongue plunges inside of me and I scream his name, my back arching off the bed as I come.

When I come back to earth, Max is licking his lips, watching me with hooded eyes. He passes me a takeout container and a plastic fork before he settles next to me.

"Okay, eat. Then we're doing that again."

I smile before I take a big bite of my egg roll.

# 12

# M<sup>ax</sup>

I ADJUST myself in my jeans as I watch Sam flick through the TV channels. She's sprawled out on my couch, her tight leggings leaving nothing to the imagination. She's been teasing me for the past few weeks but it's gotten worse in the last two. She keeps sending me dirty texts or whispering what she wants to do to me in my ear whenever we make out. I've eaten her out more times than I can remember and the taste of her always drives me wild, amping up my need until I'm desperate for her.

She's driving me out of my mind but tonight marks three months and the piercing is finally healed. When she teases me tonight, there's not going to be anything stopping me from taking her.

I offered to make her dinner at my place after she got off work. She has tomorrow off and I already cleared my schedule so we have the next thirty-six hours or so to be together.

This is the first time that Sam has been to my place. I live on the opposite side of town from Eye Candy Ink and her place, so most nights when I meet her after work, we just go to her apartment. I gave her the tour earlier, of the downstairs anyway. Upstairs is just bathrooms and bedrooms and I wasn't sure that I could control myself if she was anywhere near a bed.

Downstairs is a chef's kitchen, living room, and den. The floor plan is pretty open so you can see the kitchen from the living room and the den is tucked away in the back corner behind the stairs. Everything is modern and done up in black and white and I smile when I see that the only spot of color here is Sam. Just like in my life.

She's finally settled on a TV show, some nature documentary and she's resting her head in her hands as she lays on the couch. She had offered to help me cook dinner but I wanted to spoil her. I've got just about everything ready and I start plating up the food and carrying it over to the kitchen table.

Sam sees me and shuts the TV off as she makes her way over to the table. I watch the way her hips sway and my mouth waters but it's not the food that I'm hungry for.

"This looks delicious," she says, kissing my cheek before she drops down into a chair.

"Thanks," I say, taking the chair next to her.

We eat and talk about how work was and what we have planned for next week but throughout it all, there's an underlying current. A tension that means we both know what's happening after dinner.

We both eat quickly, finishing off our tacos in record time. Sam asks to use the bathroom and I think nothing of it, watching her walk upstairs as I finish cleaning up the dishes from dinner. When she's not back down by the time that I've turned the dishwasher on, I go in search of her. All of the bedroom and bathroom doors upstairs are open except for the master bedroom. My bedroom. I head that way and as I get closer, I hear voices and what sounds like moaning coming from inside.

Sweat breaks out on my forehead and I curl my fingers into my palms before I reach for the doorknob and walk inside. Sam is spread out on the bed, naked, her hand between her legs. Her clothes are in a pile next to the bed and she's sitting up against the headboard. Her hair, dyed a bright magenta purple is like a light, drawing me closer. That's when I see that my laptop is open next to her, a porn playing on the screen.

I freeze in my tracks, watching as the girl on screen deep throats the guys big cock. The girl moans and Sam does too. My own cock stiffens in my pants and I start to feel a little dizzy. The couple moves and the girl gets on all fours, her big tits bouncing as the guy mounts her from behind and starts to pump into her.

Sam moans louder, her fingers moving over her clit, rubbing the slick folds as she watches the couple on screen. My control snaps and I start pulling at my own clothes, desperate to be naked with her. I crawl onto the bed between her thighs, kneeling there as I take her in, spread out beneath me. She moves then, getting onto her hands and knees too.

"What are you doing, Samantha?" I ask as she prowls closer to me.

She gives me a saucy smile.

"What does it look like?" She asks as she reaches over and rewinds the video to when the girl first starts blowing the guy. As the girl licks up the guy's cock, Sam takes my cock in hand, running her fingers up my length before she opens her mouth wide and gives the tip a lick. She flicks the ring in the tip of my cock and my balls tighten up. The piercing adds a whole new sensation and I wonder how it will feel once I'm inside of her tight pussy. She sucks the head into her mouth, rolling the piercing with her tongue and my head tilts back, but not for long. Watching her blow me is too enticing.

My hands find their way into her hair and I groan when she takes me further into her mouth, mimicking what's happening on screen. Sam moans, using her hand to stroke the part that she can't fit in her mouth. She can't deep throat me like the girl on screen but I am bigger than that guy. Besides, deep throating me isn't what has me so hot. It's the fact that it's her, it's Sam and that's what has made me hotter than I've ever been in my life. I don't need a porn star. I just need Sam.

As the video changes to fucking, Sam shifts back, licking her lips as she pops my cock out of her mouth. She lays back against the pillows and spreads her legs wide in invitation, her hand finding its way back to her clit.

"Are you trying to tease me?" I ask as I prowl closer to her.

"Am I teasing you? It looks like I'm here, wet and ready for you."

I crawl between her spread thighs, meeting her eyes as I fist my cock and start to stroke myself in time with her movements. The porno is just background noise as we watch each other, sexual tension filling the air until I can't stand it any longer. I can tell that Sam is close but I don't want her to come just yet. I don't want her to come until I'm buried deep inside of her.

"Are you ready for me?" I ask, playing with the piercing in my cock. "Or do you want to finish watching your porn?"

"I'm ready for you, Max." She says as she spreads her legs even wider, showing me the puffy pink folds that are begging for my touch, my mouth, my cock. "This was just another test. I just wanted to see what you would do," she says, laying back even more against the pillows.

"Well, let me show you."

# 13

---

S am

MAX MOVES QUICK, taking over just like I knew he would. He's such a control freak and I had wondered if that would transfer into the bedroom. He finds some ties and returns to the bed, tying my hands and feet to the bedposts of his bed and I should probably be nervous but all I feel is excitement. I'm so turned on that I think I might come as soon as he touches me.

He grabs another tie before he crawls onto the bed. I'm spread out before him, completely at his mercy and I can feel my juices slipping down to pool on the bed beneath me. Max straddles me, leaning down and brushing his lips against mine in a feather soft kiss. I try to raise my head, chasing after his lips but he pulls back further.

He grabs the last tie and wraps it around my eyes,

blocking out the rest of the world so that all I can smell, taste, hear, and feel is him.

"You've been teasing me for weeks. All of those sexy texts, all of that dirty talk whenever we're alone. I'm going to make up for it now, Samantha."

His words have the insides of my thighs slickening with my desire and I bite my bottom lip, trying to hold back a moan. I can feel his warm breath on my face as he leans over me and my lips part, begging him to claim them in a kiss.

He bypasses my mouth though, trailing feather soft kisses down my neck to my shoulder. He licks over my collarbone and then surprises me when he bites down. I gasp, my body tensing and I pull against my binds. He chuckles lowly and I feel the vibrations against my skin.

He licks a trail down between my breasts and I squirm, my breath coming out in pants as my blood heats. My nipples are tight and when I feel Max's warm mouth wrap around one stiff peak and I almost come off the bed. My back arches and I moan as I pull against the ties. I want to beg him to take me already, to fill me until I'm so stuffed with his cock that I feel like I can't breathe.

He sucks on my tits, switching back and forth until I'm a trembling mess beneath him. He pulls on the rings through my nipples and with each tug I feel an answering pulse between my thighs. I'm so wet that I think I might come from him playing with my tits alone. I hear moaning and I realize that the porn is still playing on the laptop next to us.

Max shifts on top of me, kissing his way down my body until he's between my legs.

"Hmm, so wet," he murmurs as his finger slides down my center.

"Please, Max!" I cry out, more turned on then I've ever been in my life.

"I love hearing you say my name like that, but I'm not quite done with you yet."

I moan and writhe and at one point scream as he drives me out of my mind with his mouth. He licks up my core, drinking down my juices before he circles my clit, flicking the barbell over and over as he pushes one thick finger inside of me.

When he curls his finger, rubbing against that spot inside of me that he knows drives me wild and tugs on the barbell in my clit, I lose it, falling over the edge and screaming out his name as I go. I'm not aware of anything after that, just blackness as my pleasure floods through me. I feel the bed shift and then Max is thrusting into me.

Feeling his piercing drag inside of me as he stretches me has me coming again. I pull against the ties as Max fills me to the point of pain but that sting only drives me higher, prolonging my orgasm.

He sets off on a punishing pace and I can tell that he's close to his release as well. The harder he fucks me, the wetter I get. My pussy squelches as he pounds into me and when he takes one nipple into his mouth and tugs on the ring, I come again.

I must black out because the next thing I know, Max is untying me and removing the blindfold. I lay on the bed boneless as he closes the laptop and sets in on the bedside table. He spoons behind me, pulling me against him as he nuzzles his face into my hair.

I close my eyes, smiling as he lets out a deep breath.

"I love you, Samantha."

"I love you too, Max," I say before my eyes fall closed and I drift off to sleep.

## 14

# M ax

I'M in the middle of a conference call the next week when Sam burst into my office in the back of Abernathy Brewhouse. The door slams back against the wall and I jerk in my chair, eyes wide as I turn to see what's wrong. Sam is standing in the door frame, panting, her face red and a little sweaty, but her eyes are wild with excitement.

"You have to come with me!" She says, hurrying around the desk and grabbing my arm.

She tugs on my arm and I hurry to end my phone call.

"I'll have to call you back. Something has come up," I say before I hit end and grab my car keys off my desk.

"What's going on?" I ask as I hurry to keep up with her.

She doesn't look hurt and if something was wrong then she would look scared or worried, not excited.

"Atlas and Darcy are getting married!"

"Today? As in right now?" I ask, trying to catch up.

"Yeah, his parents couldn't come up from Philadelphia. Big surprise, right?" She says, rolling her eyes.

"So where are they getting married then?"

"The courthouse. In like twenty minutes! We have to hurry!"

Sam is practically skipping as we head out to my car. I get her door for her and then race around the hood. We speed off toward the courthouse and Sam tells me how excited she is. She says she knew that Atlas would be the first of the Eye Candy Ink crew to get married, that he and Darcy are perfect for each other. I listen to her chatter, as we battle traffic downtown to the courthouse.

I have to circle the lot twice before I finally find a spot and then I grab Sam's hand and we sprint up the steps and into the courthouse. We find the right office and hurry inside. Sam and I are the last to arrive and I smile when I see Zeke and Nico sitting in the chairs along the far wall. Zeke is staring at his phone, a soft smile playing on his lips. Sam told me that some girl came in to see him last week and he's seemed off ever since. I'm dying to ask him about it but now doesn't seem like the right time or place for that.

Mischa has his hand interlocked with a pretty black-haired girl with the brightest purple eyes that I've ever seen. He's grinning like the lunatic that he is as he spins her out and then tugs her back into his side. She's laughing and her grin matches his. That must be Indie.

Atlas is standing with his bride to be beside them. Darcy is a curvy girl who is watching Indie and Mischa with a bright smile. She's wearing a white sundress with some flowers in her hair. She's cuddled up against him and he's staring down at her like she's his everything. I know that look well. I tug Sam into my side as we walk over to join them.

We only wait a minute before Atlas and Darcy's names are called and we all file back into a smaller room. Mischa and Indie serve as best man and maid of honor and the rest of us stand against the back wall. The ceremony is over quickly and we all cheer as they slide the rings on and then kiss.

"Soon, that will be us," I whisper in Sam's ear and she smirks at me.

"Don't count on it."

I grin, remembering how she said that to me the first night we met. Atlas and Darcy turn and both are beaming as they walk back to us and we head out the front door. I had offered to take them out anywhere but apparently their first date was at Abernathy Brewhouse and so we headed there. I tell them that dinner is on me as we head into the private room in the back. Mischa cheers and Nico just rolls his eyes.

We spend the rest of the night eating and drinking until we're stuffed. We laugh and talk about our plans for the future, toasting the new married couple until everyone's eyes start to droop. At the end of the night, we all say good-bye. I watch as Mischa ushers Indie into his car and wave at Zeke and Nico as they head over to their cars. Someone, probably Mischa and Indie, tied cans to the bumper of Atlas's car and he and Darcy laugh when they see it. He kisses her as he tucks her into the car and I realize that he hasn't stopped smiling all day.

I help Sam into the car and I realize that I haven't stopped smiling all afternoon either.

## 15

# M<sup>ax</sup>

**FIVE YEARS LATER...**

"Do you think mom is going to be mad?"

I look down at my daughter, smiling slightly. We got married about six months after Atlas did and found out that Sam was pregnant a month after that. Our daughter, Catherine 'Cat' Schulz was born nine months later.

I had asked her dad and both of her brothers before I proposed. I had anticipated it being a fight and prepared this whole speech about how no one would ever love her as much as me but in the end they gave me their blessing right away. Her dad even said that he had been expecting it sooner.

Sam had cried when she said yes and to this day, it's

been the only time that I've seen her cry. Although, she did shed a tear or two when Cat was born.

We took turns bringing Cat with us to work until she started preschool last year. Uncle Zeke and Nico both missed playing with their niece and I know that Uncle Atlas and Mischa missed seeing her in the shop too.

"I think your mother would have done the same exact thing."

"Are you mad?" She asks, looking uncertain.

"Did you tell your teacher that that boy was bothering you?"

"Yeah like every single day for the past week."

"What did she do?"

"She just told me to ignore him but I couldn't cause he kept following me around and messing with me. Then she said that he just liked me but I don't like him and that's not how you show someone that you like them."

"That's right and I'll be talking to your teacher and principal about how they handled this later. You stood up for yourself, Cat. I'll never be mad at you for doing that."

She hugs my legs and I wrap my arm around her, sighing as my cell phone buzzes in my pocket. I pull it out and answer when I see my wife's name on the screen.

"Hey,"

"Hey, sorry I was with a client but I saw I had a missed call from you and from Cat's school. Is everything okay?"

"She punched that Decan kid,"

"Good."

"I knew you'd say that," I say with a smile.

"That little bastard had it coming."

"Let's try to remember that he is five, dear."

"Is she okay?"

"Yeah. We're almost to Eye Candy now," I say as we turn onto the block. "See you in a minute."

We open the door to the shop a minute later and Cat runs ahead of me. Sam already has the gate open and Cat runs into her arms.

"You okay?" She asks, kneeling down so she can check Cat over herself.

"I'm fine. Can I watch Uncle Nico tattoo?"

"Not right now, but Aunt Indie is here and she said that she would watch you for a few hours."

As if on cue, Indie and Mischa walk up from his office and Cat races over to hug them.

"Ready to go hang out for a bit?"

"Yeah!"

"Let's get some ice cream and then I'll show you some stuff."

"Alright," Cat says, taking Indie's hand and walking to the front door with her.

"Now, have you ever logged into someone's account?"

Cat shakes her head no, a grin stretching her face.

"Okay, now technically, it's called hacking," she says as she leads Cat out the door.

Mischa, Sam, and I stand in silence, watching them go.

"Should we be worried about that?" I ask.

"Probably," Mischa says with a grin as he watches his wife lead our daughter away.

Mischa heads back to his room a minute later and I turn to my wife, leaning on the front counter. Sam is still watching our daughter walk hand in hand down the street with Aunt Indie and she smiles slightly before she gets this far off look on her face.

"I wonder how she's going to take the news," she murmurs and my brow scrunches.

"What news?"

"That she's going to be a big sister," Sam says, finally turning to meet my eyes.

"Oh, you brat," I say with a grin as I lean over the counter and cradle her head in my hands. "When did you find out?"

"Last week. I wanted it to be a surprise."

"Mission accomplished."

She laughs, her whole face glowing as she beams up at me.

"Are you happy?"

"Happiest I've ever been," I promise her as I pull her closer and brush my lips against hers.

"I love you, Samantha."

"Love you more, Maxwell."

# ABOUT THE AUTHOR

## CONNECT WITH ME!

If you enjoyed this story, please consider leaving a review on Amazon or any other reader site or blog that you like. Don't forget to recommend it to your other reader friends.

If you want to chat with me, please consider joining my VIP list or connecting with me on one of my Social Media platforms. I love talking with each of my readers. Links below!

➤ VIP list
➤ shawhartbooks.com

## ALSO BY SHAW HART

Remembering Valentine's Day

Finding Their Rhythm

Her Scottish Savior

Stealing Her

Hop Stuff

**Series by Shaw Hart**

**Telltale Heart Series**

Bought and Paid For

His Miracle

Pretty Girl

**Ash Mountain Pack Series**

Growling For My Mate

Claiming My Mate

Mated For Life

Chasing My Mate

Protecting Our Mate

**Love Note Series**

Signing Off With Love

Care Package Love

Wrong Number, Right Love

**Folklore Series**

Kidnapped by Bigfoot

Loved by Yeti

Claimed by Her Sasquatch

Printed in Great Britain
by Amazon

79240069R00051